Troll and the Oliver

For Noah & Ivy,
Emily & Isabel, and Jude –
what a lovely bunch!

A TEMPLAR BOOK

First published in the UK in 2013 by Templar Publishing,
This softback edition published in the UK in 2014 by Templar Publishing,
an imprint of The Templar Company Limited,
Deepdene Lodge, Deepdene Avenue, Dorking, Surrey, RH5 4AT, UK
www.templarco.co.uk

1 3 5 7 9 10 8 6 4 2

ISBN 978-1-84877-173-4

Edited by Libby Hamilton

Printed in China

Troll and the Oliver

Adam Stower

templar publishing

This is the Troll.

And this is an Oliver.

Every day, around lunchtime…

… Troll tries to eat the Oliver.

But catching an Oliver is a tricky business.
No matter how hard Troll tried,
he could never quite manage it.

And the Oliver was never any help at all.

Instead of standing
nice and still,

the Oliver dashed about
all over the place,

which made grabbing it
very difficult.

Then each time Troll got close,

the Oliver would suddenly vanish.

And giggle.

MY NAME'S OLIVER, TEE-HEE-HEE! THAT SILLY OLD TROLL WILL NEVER FIND ME!

And for something normally so LOUD and SQUEAKY,

it would choose just the wrong moment...

Even when Troll was sure he'd finally,
definitely, ABSOLUTELY caught the Oliver...

It was always the same.

By Spring, Troll was grumpy,

tired and very, very hungry.

It just wasn't fair. It was almost as if the Oliver

was doing it on purpose.

Troll went back to his hole

and ate his dinner of twigs and stones.

He'd had enough of pesky Olivers.

The next morning, Oliver fetched
his basket and set off to go shopping as usual.
He took extra care through the woods,
expecting the Troll to jump out
at any moment.

But it didn't.

On the way back,
Oliver checked the long grass in the meadow
to see if the Troll was hiding there,
waiting to grab his ankles.

It wasn't.

Then he tiptoed across the bridge,

just in case.

But there
was no sign
of the Troll
anywhere.
It was most
peculiar.

In fact, Oliver didn't see the Troll all day long
and soon he was safely home again.

It was not until Oliver was busy in the kitchen
that he suddenly understood…

The Troll had given up!
It was gone forever!

OLIVER HAD WON!

He felt exceedingly
pleased with
himself.

Troll felt exceedingly pleased with himself.

But unluckily for Troll...

and luckily for
Olivers everywhere...

Olivers taste **REVOLTING!**

BLEEEUGHHHH!

Poor Troll.

Now he was hungrier than ever.

Troll slumped and sighed. Oliver sat and dripped.

But just then they heard a... tick, tick, tick, tick, PING!

And from that moment on, everything changed.

These days Troll is never hungry

and he won't ever have to eat stones again, or twigs...

or Olivers, thank goodness!

Author's note:

I would strongly advise the reader
to ALWAYS have a cake handy,
just in case a troll should happen by.

He might be hungry…

TROLLIVER'S COOKBOOK

Troll Cupcake Recipe

(Makes 12 cupcakes)

Ingredients

For the cupcake sponges:
- 110g/4oz butter, softened
- 110g/4oz caster sugar
- 2 eggs
- 1 tsp vanilla extract
- 110g/4oz self-raising flour

For the icing and decorations:
- 140g/5oz butter, softened
- 280g/10oz icing sugar
- A few drops of food colouring
- Dessicated coconut
- Your favourite sweets

Baking the cupcakes

- Ask a grown-up to preheat the oven to 180C/350F/Gas mark 4
- Line a cupcake tin with 12 paper cases
- Stir the butter and sugar together in a bowl to make a smooth, pale mixture
- Beat in the eggs a little at a time and stir in the vanilla extract (you might need some troll-help for the beating - it means stirring really hard and fast)

- Mix in the flour using a big metal spoon
- Spoon the mixture into the paper cases until they are half full
- Ask a grown-up to put them into the oven and bake them for 10-15 minutes, until golden brown on top
- Let them cool in the cupcake tray for 10 minutes, then let them cool on a wire cooling rack

Making the icing

- Beat the butter in a big bowl until it is soft
- Add half the icing sugar and beat until it is smooth
- Add the other half of the icing sugar and do the same
- Add the food colouring

Decorating your cupcake

- Cover each cupcake with icing
- Put the dessicated coconut and food colouring in a bowl and mix
- Press each cupcake, upside down, into the bowl of coconut to give it troll fur. (If you don't like coconut, just use a fork to make your icing stick up like fur!)
- Add sweets to make your troll face - chocolate buttons, raisins and liquorice work well!

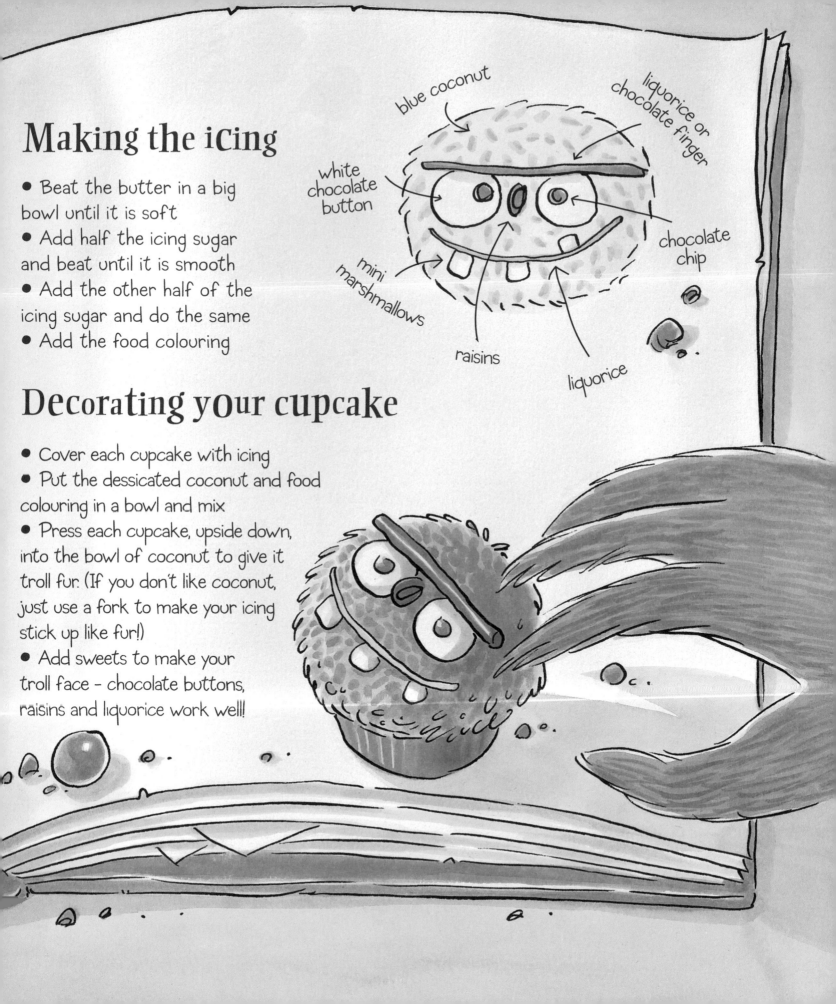

blue coconut

liquorice or chocolate finger

white chocolate button

chocolate chip

mini marshmallows

raisins

liquorice

Praise for Troll and the Oliver

"As monster books go this is pretty much perfect... the double-punch payoff is so utterly, deliciously satisfying that for a tiny, tiny moment your little one will sit agog."
—Read it, Daddy!

"Excellent clever plot, amusing detailed illustrations and a pleasing twist at the end."
—Peters Books (Book of the Week)

"Troll is wonderfully depicted with the most amazingly expressive eyebrows you have ever seen!"
—Parents in Touch Magazine